The Berenstain Bears'
Family Reunion

by Stan & Jan Berenstain
with Mike Berenstain

HarperCollins*Publishers*

I'm happy that we have good weather for our family get-together!

Dear Parent:
Your child's love of reading starts here!

Every child learns to read in a different way and at his or her own speed. Some go back and forth between reading levels and read favorite books again and again. Others read through each level in order. You can help your young reader improve and become more confident by encouraging his or her own interests and abilities. From books your child reads with you to the first books he or she reads alone, there are I Can Read Books for every stage of reading:

SHARED READING
Basic language, word repetition, and whimsical illustrations, ideal for sharing with your emergent reader

BEGINNING READING
Short sentences, familiar words, and simple concepts for children eager to read on their own

READING WITH HELP
Engaging stories, longer sentences, and language play for developing readers

READING ALONE
Complex plots, challenging vocabulary, and high-interest topics for the independent reader

ADVANCED READING
Short paragraphs, chapters, and exciting themes for the perfect bridge to chapter books

I Can Read Books have introduced children to the joy of reading since 1957. Featuring award-winning authors and illustrators and a fabulous cast of beloved characters, I Can Read Books set the standard for beginning readers.

A lifetime of discovery begins with the magical words "I Can Read!"

Visit www.icanread.com for information
on enriching your child's reading experience.

The Berenstain Bears' Family Reunion Copyright © 2009 by Berenstain Bears, Inc. All rights reserved. Manufactured in China. No part of this book may be used or reproduced in any manner whatsoever without written permission except in the case of brief quotations embodied in critical articles and reviews. For information address HarperCollins Children's Books, a division of HarperCollins Publishers, 195 Broadway, New York, NY 10007. www.icanread.com

Library of Congress Cataloging-in-Publication Data is available.
ISBN 978-0-06-058359-0 (trade bdg.) — ISBN 978-0-06-058360-6 (pbk.)

❖
First Edition
16 17 18 SCP 10 9 8

Who is coming to
our family party,
Cousin Jill and
Uncle Artie?

Yes! We'll see Grizzly Gramps
and Gran, of course,
Great Aunt Min and Cousin Morse.

Aunts and uncles, nephews, nieces
will come together like puzzle pieces.

We do indeed have good weather.

But are we ready for our get-together?

We've done our best to prepare
to welcome the family to our lair.

We've borrowed chairs
from miles around.
We've had our yard
wired for sound.

We've lots of room for cars to park.

We've put up lights for when it's dark.

We've lots and lots of food and drink.

Yes, we are prepared, I think.

Everyone's coming to the party!

There's Cousin Jill and Uncle Artie!

Grizzly Gramps and Gran, of course!

Great Aunt Min and Cousin Morse!

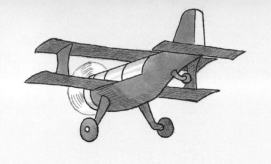

Look! Twin Cousins Mike and Ike
are riding their two-seater bike.
Look out! Aunt Jane and Cousin Klute
are coming down by parachute!

Here come more in cars and buses!

And a great big truck! It's Uncle Gus's!

We shout hello! We kiss! We hug!

We pass around the honey jug!

Papa Bear and Uncle Mack

slap each other on the back.

We take pictures of each other.

Here's me with Honey, Sis, Pa,

and Mother.

We dance, we sing, and we laugh at jokes.

It's fun to be with family folks!

Then we eat, and eat, and eat, and eat!

Our family feast cannot be beat!

Now we hear from Great-Aunt Bess,

"All right, you bears, clean up this mess!"

Then all is quiet. All is calm.

The bears line up to thank our mom.

She gets a gift from Cousin Heather
to thank her for the get-together!

Thank You,
Mama
Bear

We say good-bye. We kiss. We hug.

We finish off the honey jug.

Back into cars and into buses.

Back in the truck that's Uncle Gus's.

Our get-together now is done.

Thank you for coming, everyone!

We hope that you had FUN! FUN! FUN!